RAGGEDY ANN
And the
HAPPY MEADOW

RAGGEDY ANN
and the
HAPPY MEADOW
by JOHNNY GRUELLE

A YEARLING BOOK

YEARLING BOOKS are designed especially to entertain and enlighten young
people. The finest available books for children have been selected under
the direction of Charles F. Reasoner, Professor of Elementary Education,
New York University.

For a complete listing of all Yearling titles, write to Education Sales
Department, Dell Publishing Co., Inc., 1 Dag Hammarskjold Plaza,
New York, N.Y. 10017.

Published by
Dell Publishing Co., Inc.
1 Dag Hammarskjold Plaza
New York, New York 10017

WORTH GRUELLE

THE FAIRIES' CURE

FOR A LONG TIME, Raggedy Ann and Raggedy Andy had wandered through the deep, deep woods, filled with fairies and everything, searching for adventures. The little rag dolls, made of cloth and stuffed with soft white cotton, had found many exciting adventures and had made lots of new friends. Many things happened to them too which they had not expected. Witches and Wizards had tried to capture them, and they had seen such things as flying boats and magic Hobby Horses: Most of the time they had great fun, although at other times they had cause for worry. But they were always happy with their wide smiles painted on their faces; although, even if their smiles had not been painted on, they would have been cheerful and friendly anyway.

On this day, though, they wandered out of the deep, deep woods, and came to a beautiful meadow, flooded with yellow sunshine. The emerald green grass swayed in the soft, perfumed breezes and the

many-colored flowers seemed to be curtseying and bowing as a welcome to the little rag dolls. Naturally too, the air was filled with the songs of different birds happily going about their business of building nests, teaching baby birds how to fly, and how to get food and oh! so many other things. Raggedy Ann and Raggedy Andy looked cheerfully at each other and then at the meadow with wonder. They had thought the deep, deep woods were surely the most beautiful spot in the world. And now they found that, here in the meadow, there was a different kind of supreme beauty which Mother Nature was showing them. Their hearts were so full that they did not want to say anything to spoil the magic spell which seemed to be cast over them. So they walked along silently, finding many things they had never before seen.

Suddenly, a little yellow Wild Canary flew past the Raggedys and landed on a tall weed right in front of them. But as he did so, he sat on one foot and held the other close to his body as if it pained him.

"You speak to him, Raggedy Ann," whispered

Raggedy Andy. "Your voice is softer than mine and you will not frighten him away. Maybe some naughty boy has thrown a stone and hurt his leg!"

The little yellow Wild Canary turned his handsome little head toward the two Raggedys and said, "Tweet! Tweet!" in the prettiest way.

"Tweet, Tweet!" Raggedy Ann replied in the same tones the little yellow Wild Canary had used. "Has someone hurt your leg, Carlie Canary?"

"Tweet, Tweeeeeeeeeeet! Tweetity Twee-ee-rrrrrr-eet! Tweet!" Carlie Canary sang. "No, Raggedy Ann," he said, "I flew up on a thorn tree and ran a sharp thorn into my foot!"

"You won't be frightened if we come close and look at it, will you?" asked Raggedy Andy.

In reply Carlie Canary flew over to Raggedy Ann's hand, which she held out when she saw him coming.

"Yes, there is a thorn in it," said Raggedy Ann. "See if you can pull it out, Raggedy Andy!"

Raggedy Andy tried to pull the thorn from Carlie Canary's foot, but Andy's hands were made almost the same as large old-fashioned mittens, and he could

7

not use his thumbs to catch hold of the tiny thorn.

"It doesn't hurt very much," said Carlie Canary bravely. "See, I can sing just as well as I always do!"

And he sang so sweetly that Raggedy Ann and Raggedy Andy had to wipe their shoe-button eyes on Ann's apron.

Finally, though, Raggedy Andy thought of a plan. He found two little flat pieces of wood, and by holding them together like Percy Pinchbug's pincers, he was able to pull the thorn from Carlie Canary's foot.

"Oh my, that feels so much better!" Carlie Canary chirped. "It makes me want to sing every song I know!"

"That makes us happy then," said Raggedy Ann. "And now if you will let me, I'll show you how every mama cures her little boy or girl who has a hurt."

And with this, Raggedy Ann kissed Carlie Canary's little foot.

"There, that did cure it; now I'm all better!" Carlie Canary cried as if he could hardly believe it. And he stood up on the foot which had had the thorn in it. "See," he chirped happily, "I can dance up and down on it and it doesn't hurt one bit!"

"It is wonderful what a kiss will do," said Raggedy Andy. "I suppose that a long time ago the Fairies must have gathered together and said, 'Let's give every mother and daddy in the world a fine present!' And they wondered what the present should be. Then one of the Fairies said, 'I know what it shall be!'

" 'What?' asked all the other pretty Fairies as they crowded around the one who had spoken.

8

WORTH GRUELLE

" 'Well, you know,' said the first Fairy, 'children are always bumping their heads, and stubbing their toes, getting scratched by kitties, and always getting little hurts of one kind or another. Let's give to every mama and daddy a way to cure every little hurt their children may have.'

" 'Oh, but then we would have to make millions and millions of bottles and fill them with medicine and they would always be getting spilled, or broken, or something,' said another Fairy.

"The first little Fairy laughed her most tinkly little Fairy laugh and said, 'The cure I am talking about can be given very easily. We shall make a very, very magical sweet medicine and we shall put it on the lips of every mama and daddy in the world. Then all they will have to do is to kiss the spot that hurts their little one, and that will be the cure.'

" 'Ohhh!' and 'Ahhh!' cried all the little Fairies as they fluttered their rainbow wings with happiness. 'We shall make a charm that will never, never fail, for we will fill it with love and kindness.'

9

"And that's what the Fairies did!"

"How in the world did you know that, Raggedy Andy?" asked Raggedy Ann as she looked at Raggedy Andy in surprise to hear him tell such a sweet story. Then she laughed and laughed; and Raggedy Andy laughed and laughed; and at last Carlie Canary broke into little birdlike laughter too. For there, sitting on Raggedy Andy's shoulder was a little Gnome with long white whiskers, and he was winking his right eye at Raggedy Ann and Carlie Canary. And they knew then that the little Gnome had told the story in Raggedy Andy's voice!

"And that is why kisses cure," said the little Gnome. "For I was there and I saw the Fairies make the magic present for every mama and daddy, and it is worth more than all the gold and precious stones in the whole world."

JOHNNY CRICKET'S FIDDLE

"WHERE DID the little Gnome go?" asked Raggedy Ann. "He was here sitting on your shoulder just a moment ago, Raggedy Andy."

"I don't know," Raggedy Andy replied. "I did not feel him leave. But then, I didn't feel him come either."

"He was a darling little creature," said Raggedy Ann. "Not over two inches high when he stood straight up."

The two Raggedys looked about them in the tall grass and finally Raggedy Andy cried, "There he goes, Raggedy Ann—down that tiny path beneath those bending flowers."

"He's chasing something!" Raggedy Ann exclaimed as she pushed her rag head beneath the flowers so she might look down the tiny path. "Come and see, Raggedy Andy."

Raggedy Andy could see, when he got down beside Raggedy Ann, that indeed the little Gnome was chasing something. In and out among the flower stems and grass blades he darted, while just ahead of him jumped another tiny creature. To the little Gnome and the tiny creature, the stems of the flowers and the blades of grass were as big as a great forest of trees would seem to a real boy or girl. Every once in a while the little Gnome would stub his toe over a tiny twig or root, but he would get up and start running again.

The two Raggedys crawled through the flowers and the grass, and they followed the little Gnome until they got a good look at the creature he was so busy chasing.

"Oh, it is Johnny Cricket!" Raggedy Ann cried. "I wonder why the little Gnome is chasing him."

Johnny Cricket dodged this way and that, around stems of weeds and over tiny sticks and pebbles, until he came to a tiny hole, and *whoosh,* he crawled into it as quickly as he could. The little Gnome came to the tiny hole into which Johnny Cricket had disappeared and he sat down on a little pebble near by.

"He won't be down there very long," he said with a laugh, when he saw Raggedy Ann and Raggedy Andy watching him. "He will probably bump right into Arthur Angleworm and Arthur will wiggle Johnny Cricket right up out of the hole again."

Sure enough, this was what happened. Arthur Angleworm's front hall was so small that Johnny Cricket could not turn around in it, and so when he came out, he had to back out. The little Gnome caught Johnny Cricket's long legs and pulled him out. Then he put Johnny Cricket across his knee and paddled him until Johnny Cricket squeaked and squeaked.

"Why do you paddle Johnny Cricket?" Raggedy Ann wished to know.

The little Gnome held Johnny Cricket by his coat-tails and pulled him up on Raggedy Ann's nice clean white apron.

"Ask Johnny Cricket." The little Gnome laughed. "He knows why, and he knows he deserved every paddle I gave him. Don't you, Johnny Cricket?"

Johnny Cricket wiggled his eyebrows in a funny way and twisted one toe around before he replied, "Yes, I did deserve every paddle, and I am so sorry too! You see, a while ago, I fell off a tall weed and landed right on my back and broke my fiddle. When I saw Charlie Cricket fast asleep under the toadstool, I took his fiddle and put my broken one in its place."

"My, oh my!" was all Raggedy Ann could say.

"Yes, I know it was wrong," Johnny Cricket squeaked. "I knew it just as soon as I had taken Charlie's fiddle, but the little Gnome started chasing me before I had a chance to put Charlie's fiddle back and take my own."

"Dear me, I'm sorry I did not know that!" the little Gnome said. "But here comes Charlie Cricket now, and you can see that he has been crying."

"I broke my fiddle!" Charlie Cricket squeaked when he saw the little Gnome. "Will you please fix it for me?"

"That was my fiddle," said Johnny Cricket, as he pulled Charlie's fiddle out from under his coat and

15

handed it to Charlie. "It was naughty of me to take your fiddle, Charlie, and I am sorry."

"Well, please don't cry, Johnny Cricket!" Charlie said as he took his own little fiddle and wiped Johnny's eyes with his pocket hanky. "I forgive you."

"I shall never, never do anything like that again," Johnny Cricket cried in his tiny cricket voice, and the wee cricket tears came from his eyes and trickled down on his necktie.

"Well well, well!" The little Gnome laughed as he put his arm around Johnny Cricket. "Let me see the broken fiddle."

And with six short magic words the little Gnome fixed Johnny Cricket's fiddle so that it played as sweetly as ever.

Johnny Cricket was now as happy as Charlie Cricket and he laughed through his tears. Then he and Charlie Cricket tuned up their tiny fiddles and started to play gay little cricket tunes while the little Gnome danced and kicked up his heels on Raggedy Ann's apron.

Aunt Cynthia Cricket came up just then with a basket of delicious cricket cookies and gave some to the two Cricket boys and the little Gnome.

"I shall never, never take anything that does not belong to me again," Johnny said, with his mouth full of cricket cookies. "For that would make someone else unhappy, and when I have made another creature unhappy, then I am unhappy too."

THE PAPER MAKERS

RAGGEDY ANN and Raggedy Andy stood looking at a queer little ball hanging on a tall weed.

"Whatever in the wide, wide, beautiful world can it be?" Raggedy Andy wondered as he caught hold of the weed stem and bent it over so that the queer little ball came down near his head. "There's a hole in the bottom and it looks as though anything inside would roll right out," he added.

Raggedy Andy shook the weed stem once, and something inside the queer little ball rattled about and then came popping out, striking Raggedy Andy right between his shoe-button eyes, *powie!*

"Aha!" Raggedy Ann laughed. "You deserved that, Raggedy Andy."

"Are they bees?" Raggedy Andy asked.

"No, we are not bees," said the tiny creature who had hit Raggedy Andy between his shoe-button eyes. "We are hornets, and that is our house, and you rattled the dishes off our cupboard shelves. That's why I hit you between your shoe-button eyes."

18

"Dear me!" Raggedy Andy smiled. "I am sorry I did that. I hope the dishes were not broken, Henny Hornet."

Henny Hornet went into his tiny house and then came out again. "It's all right, Raggedy Andy. Not one was broken."

"I'm very glad," said Raggedy Ann. "Where do you get your little dishes, Henny Hornet?"

"We make them," Henny Hornet replied. "Henrietta and I. Here comes Henrietta now. This is Raggedy Ann and Raggedy Andy," Henny Hornet introduced them to Henriettta Hornet.

"I'm pleased to meet you," said Henrietta Hornet

as she picked up her skirts and made a curtsy.

"And we're pleased to meet *you*," said Raggedy Andy and Raggedy Ann.

"I just rattled the weed stem and shook most of the dishes off your cupboard shelves," said Raggedy Andy, "and I am very, very sorry!"

Henrietta Hornet laughed. "Well, you couldn't break the dishes anyway. They are made of paper."

"Paper?" the two Raggedys exclaimed in surprise.

"Oh, yes!" Henrietta Hornet laughed. "Didn't you know that, Raggedy Ann and Raggedy Andy? Why, our whole house is made of paper, too. The Hornet family is noted for being the first paper makers. A long time ago grown-up people watched hornets chew up wood into fine pulp and plaster it together to make the hornet houses. That is how the grown-up people learned to grind up trees and make the pulp into paper. Much later, they learned to use the paper to print pretty little picture books, and newspapers and other things like that."

"You must be very proud to know that your long-long-time-ago hornet Grampies and Grammies were of so much help to grown-up people," said Raggedy Ann.

"We are very, very glad of it." Henrietta Hornet laughed. "But it does not make us proud." Then, turning her head, she asked Henny Hornet, "Was that the baby squeaking?"

"I believe it was," Henny Hornet answered as he flew into his little paper house. Soon he came out with baby Helen Hornet.

"You rattled the house so much that the crib turned over," said Henny Hornet to Raggedy Andy. "Helen was down underneath the crib laughing and squeaking and playing with her toes."

"I shall be more careful the next time I want to know about something," Raggedy Andy said. "Many times, I am afraid, when we want to know about other people's business, we do forget to think about their wishes first. Then there can be trouble."

"Yes, indeed." Raggedy Ann laughed as she watched the little bald baby, Helen Hornet, wink her large yellow eyes. "We all want to know why things happen as they do, and how things work. But instead of just shaking everything and everybody up, helter-skelter, first we must make sure we will do no great damage."

Raggedy Andy thought for a while and then added, "Often children get into trouble just because they do not ask their mothers and daddies first about things. And the funny part of it is, that if they did ask first, most often mother or daddy would be happy to ex-

21

plain how, and why, and where, and when! Then the children would not get into trouble."

Just then baby Hornet blinked her big yellow eyes as if to say, "I shall try to remember that, Raggedy Andy. I truly shall try!"

THE BUTTERCUP STORY

"IT SEEMS a shame to pick the pretty flowers from their homes," Raggedy Ann said. "See how beautiful they are with their golden yellow heads shining in the sun."

"They make very pretty crowns when you braid their stems together," Raggedy Andy said.

"Yes, Raggedy Andy, but each little flower is growing on a stem, and that stem is on a larger stem, so there are many flowers joined together. Who knows but that each little plant is a family and each little flower a brother or sister? Then, you see, if we pick one little flower from the family, the others must miss his happy, bright-colored face."

"Your sweet candy heart makes you think of so many kindly things," Raggedy Andy said as he got down on his hands and knees and looked closely at the clusters of flower families.

Presently old Granpa Skeeter Hawk flew up and landed on Raggedy Ann's shoulder.

"We are watching the pretty little golden buttercups," Raggedy Ann told Granpa Skeeter Hawk. "They are nodding on their stems just as if they were talking to one another."

"Maybe they are." Granpa Skeeter Hawk chuckled. "But their voices are so soft that even I cannot hear them."

"Each flower looks as though it had been painted with varnish," Raggedy Andy said. "It is so shiny!"

"Yes, they are shiny," Granpa Skeeter Hawk said, "and that's because they are made out of Fairy gold."

"I thought Fairy gold was hard, just as other gold is," Raggedy Ann said.

"Oh dear, no," Granpa Skeeter Hawk hastened to say. "Some Fairy gold is very soft and turns into happy singing, and other Fairy gold is soft and spreads over the surface of things, making them shiny, as it has done for these buttercups. You know, at one time, all of the flowers were white."

"We didn't know that, Granpa Skeeter Hawk!" exclaimed Raggedy Ann and Raggedy Andy in surprise.

"Oh, yes, indeed. At least that is what Grampy Hoppytoad says, and he is very, very old and very, very wise. Grampy Hoppytoad says that a long time ago the buttercups grew high up on the hills where they could look far out over the rim of the world. And they turned their little white faces to the East each morning as they nodded and whispered 'Good morning' to Mister Sun.

"One night when Mister Sun had gone around to visit the other side of the world, the little gnomes, who lived and worked down inside the high hill where the white buttercups grew, dug so much dirt out from under the hill that the whole top of the hill slid off and went rolling down into the valley. At first, they did not realize that the little white buttercups were buried under the earth and were mixed up with pebbles and dirt. And before they had a chance to do anything about it, Mister Sun peeped out and asked, 'Why, where are my pretty little flower friends who greet me each morning?' And the little gnomes heard him and told him just what had happened.

"Then Mister Sun asked, 'If my pretty little flower friends are buried down beneath the soil, won't you little gnomes dig them out, so I may see them?'

"Of course the little gnomes were always glad to do things to help others, and especially to help old Mister Sun. So they came marching up out of the hill with their picks and shovels, and before Mister Sun's beams were directly over them, they had taken the little buttercups from beneath the stones and dirt and planted them along the edge of the brook.

"You see," Granpa Skeeter Hawk continued, "their little faces had become so dirty, and the gnomes thought the mist from the brook would wash them clean before long. But, when the Fairies who lived in the brook saw how dirty the little flower faces were, they came with spray and dashed it over the

flowers; and when the dirt was washed off, the little gnomes and old Mister Sun were quite surprised. Each little flower, instead of having a white face, was covered with the Fairy gold! And, from that day to this, they have really been little Fairy Golden Cups.

"But," Granpa Skeeter Hawk explained as he hopped up in the air and caught a mosquito, "most people do not know all this, and they call them 'buttercups'."

"Oh look!" Raggedy Andy exclaimed. "They are nodding their heads as if to say, 'Yes, yes'!"

Granpa Skeeter Hawk made his gauze wings hum, he laughed so hard. "Just you dip your hands in the

brook and wash the dust off your shoe-button eyes," he said as he flew away.

Although Raggedy Ann and Raggedy Andy did not understand what Granpa Skeeter Hawk meant, they dipped their hands into the brook and cleaned their shoe-button eyes with their wet hands.

And then, when they looked at the little Fairy Golden Cups, they knew what Granpa Skeeter Hawk was laughing about. With their brook-washed eyes, they could see what they had never seen before. In each little golden buttercup was a tiny Fairy, sitting and kicking her ever so tiny feet as if she were in a swing.

Of course, this was what was making all the buttercups nod on their stems!

THE MEADOW TELEPHONE LINES

As RAGGEDY ANN and Raggedy Andy sat in the grass down in the Happy Meadow, they could see two little spiders jumping about from one blade of grass to another.

"Just see how carefully and beautifully the spiders spin their webs," said Raggedy Andy.

"Yes, they are beautiful," said Raggedy Ann. "But they do not look very strong. If a big gust of wind came along, I imagine it could blow the web down easily."

Just then a tiny little voice close to Raggedy Ann's head asked, "But don't you know what they are doing?"

Raggedy Ann, looking up, saw a dear little Meadow Elf only two inches high, sitting on a swaying weed and swinging back and forth.

At first the Raggedys were so surprised they could not say anything. Then they both said "no" very softly.

"Well, I'll tell you." The little Meadow Elf laughed a teeny, tinkly Elfin laugh. "Those little spiders are the tiny creatures' telephone linemen, and they are stringing the telephone lines from one little village to another, so that the small creatures in the Happy Meadow may talk to one another without having to walk far."

"I never thought of such a thing," Raggedy Andy said.

"Yes, indeed," the little Meadow Elf said. "Haven't you ever noticed early in the morning, after a heavy dew, that the grass is covered with fine spider webs? Well, the spiders stretch the lines great distances and they are most plainly seen when they are covered with dew!"

"Yes, we have seen them many times," Raggedy Ann replied. "But we never thought that they were anything special."

"Well," said the little Meadow Elf, "those are telephone lines stretching from one very small village to another. It makes it very nice for Ladybugs, for instance, if any of the children get the Ladybug tummyache. Instead of Daddy Ladybug having to fly for the doctor, all he has to do is to ring the little Bluebell telephone, and soon the doctor is there to give little Baby Ladybug a spoonful of honey. Now you see how important the meadow telephone lines are."

Raggedy Ann and Raggedy Andy sat and listened without saying a word. If their smiles had not been painted on their happy faces, they would have been wider than ever. They waited for the gay little

Meadow Elf to tell them more about the telephone lines, and in a moment, the Elf continued with his story.

"Why, just the other day Mama Ladybug said to little Willie Ladybug, 'Willie, please run down to the Junebug grocery and get me a sack of flour, a dozen eggs and a bottle of milk. I want to bake a cake for supper.'

"So Willie Ladybug hopped on his little tricycle and, with a basket on the handlebar and fifteen Bugpennies in his pocket, he went spinning down the path toward the Junebug grocery. But when Willie Ladybug got to the large grown-up people's path, a boy and a girl came along and stepped right on Willie's tricycle. Willie just managed to jump off and onto the little boy's shoe where he stayed until he was carried to their house.

"Well, sir," went on the little Meadow Elf, "when Willie Ladybug did not return with the groceries, Mama Ladybug called up Aunt Jennie Junebug and asked if Willie Ladybug had started home yet. And Aunt Jennie Junebug said, 'My goodness, Mama Ladybug, he hasn't been here at all!' So then Mama Ladybug telephoned all round to everyone to find out where Willie was.

"I hunted everywhere for Willie and finally I flew by the home of the little boy and girl. I heard some-one say, 'Ladybug, Ladybug, fly away home! Your house is on fire and your children will burn!' Of course, they did not know that the Ladybug that they had was Willie Ladybug, just a little tiny boy Lady-bug. And poor little Willie's heart was going pitty-pat so fast he did not know what to do. So I flew up to him and whispered, 'Spread your wings and fly out the window.' The two children could not see me, so when Willie Ladybug flew out the window, they

thought he was flying home to his children. Ha, ha, ha!"

And the little Meadow Elf laughed so hard he lost his balance and fell right into Raggedy Ann's apron pocket. But Raggedy Ann gently took him out and put him in her lap.

After taking off his little hat to see if the feather was broken, he continued his story: "So as soon as we got out of sight, we flew down into the grass, and I called up Mama Ladybug. 'I've got Willie! We're coming right home,' I told her. It took us a long time to fly back home, but we got there before the light-

ning-bug boys lit the Teeny Town street lamps and then everyone was happy.

"Daddy Ladybug had gone to shop at the Junebug's grocery store, and we had lovely cookies, honeydew ice cream, and Junebug lollipops for supper; and I stayed all night with the Ladybugs.

"Hello," cried the little Meadow Elf. "There goes my telephone bell now!" And with a whisk he was up and away over the tall grass toward his home in the wild rosebushes.

Raggedy Ann and Raggedy Andy looked at each other, and then at the little spider boys putting up

the telephone wires, and each of them thought, "I shall be careful after this to see that I never brush the spider telephone lines down when I walk through the Happy Meadow."

TILLIE TOAD AND HER NEW CLOTHES

"Why, Tillie Toad, what are you crying for?" Raggedy Ann asked as she picked up Tillie and held the toad in her rag hands.

"Blub, blub, blub," cried the little toad as though her heart would break.

"Pat her on the back," suggested Raggedy Andy. "Maybe she has swallowed an acorn and is choking."

"Blub, blub, blub," Tillie Toad sobbed as she pointed with her little hands to her bonnet and dress. Raggedy Ann took the corner of her apron and gently wiped the tears from Tillie's eyes.

"Now tell us what the trouble is, Tillie Toad, or I'll spank you!" Raggedy Ann tried to say this very severely, but her cottony voice was so soft and her smile was so cheery, Tillie Toad knew that Raggedy Ann was just fooling.

Tillie could not help but smile a bit herself, even though there were still tears in her eyes. "You've never spanked anyone, Raggedy Ann," she said.

"Anyway, your nice soft hands would not hurt a bit."

"Now," said Raggedy Andy, "if Tillie Toad has stopped her *blub, blub, blub-ing,* we can find out why she is crying."

"Oh, I'll tell you," said Tillie Toad. "And I'll try not to *blub, blub* any more. But, you see, I get so very, very tired of wearing the same little brown bonnet and the same little brown dress all the time. If I could only change to a nice striped green and yellow dress like the one Gertrude Greenfrog is wearing, I'd be so happy."

And as Tillie sighed a very sad sigh, one little tear crept down her cheek.

"Gracious me." Raggedy Andy laughed. "You are only a year or two old, Tillie Toad, and you are already unhappy with your pretty bonnet and dress. Why, Raggedy Ann and I have worn the same clothes for fifty years or more!"

"Well," Tillie Toad exclaimed, "you have a nice striped shirt and blue pants and a blue hat, and Raggedy Ann wears a sweet blue dress with pretty little flowers on it. Why, my dress and bonnet are just as brown as mud!"

"Now don't make fun of that good brown." Raggedy Ann laughed. "Your little dress and bonnet were given to you for a good purpose. Let's just suppose that suddenly your dress could be changed to one like mine."

Before she could go on, Tillie Toad clapped her hands together, rolled her large eyes and exclaimed, "Oh, that would be ever so nice."

And Raggedy Andy mused, "Hmmm, maybe it would be nice for her, Raggedy Ann, but I do not know how it could be done."

"But it would not be nice!" Raggedy Ann objected. "And do you want to know why? I will tell you what I believe. Supposing you have a dress like mine, blue with pretty flowers on it, and a white apron with a pocket in it and——"

"A little lace pocket hanky sticking out," Tillie Toad added.

"Now you wait a moment," Raggedy Ann has-

tened to say. "And supposing you were sitting on the muddy bank of the little meadow brook and Mister Sherman Shikepoke came flying along. He has very keen eyes as you know, and if your little bonnet and dress were blue with pretty little flowers, he could see you very easily. And Mister Sherman Shikepoke would swoop down and go 'gobble-gobble.' Then where would your pretty blue dress and bonnet be? Tell me that!"

"I'd hop into the water, swim down to the bottom and hide in the mud—that's what I'd do," Tillie Toad answered.

"Ho, ho," Raggedy Andy cried. "Then he'd see your pretty dress and bonnet as plain as plain against the brown mud."

"Then I'd hide up against a tree trunk," Tillie Toad said stoutly.

"Yes, indeed." Raggedy Ann laughed softly. "That is just what you would do, Tillie Toad, and that is why dear old wise Mother Nature gave you your little brown bonnet and dress. She knew very well that if anything tried to catch you and harm you, you would either jump into the water and hide in the muddy brown bottom, or you would scoot up and hide against a tree trunk."

Raggedy Ann waited a moment while she let Tillie Toad think about this. Then she continued: "So Mother Nature has given you these brown clothes to protect you, because you are one of her workers."

"Hmmmmm!" Tillie Toad thought hard.

"Now do you understand?" Raggedy Andy asked,

quite proud of Raggedy Ann for explaining it so well to Tillie.

"Yes, I really do," Tillie Toad cheerfully said, as she wiped her eyes dry on Raggedy Ann's apron. "And I shall always be thankful to dear old wise Mother Nature that she gave me these brown clothes. Now I'm going home to explain it all to every one of my six thousand pollywog children so that when they grow up, they will never be unhappy about their brown clothes."

After thanking the two rag dolls, Tillie Toad hopped away down the little path toward the pollywog play pool in the little brook.

"You explained it just fine, Raggedy Ann," Raggedy Andy said as he put his arm lovingly around Raggedy Ann's neck.

"Oh, I only told Tillie Toad what she might have figured out if she had stopped to think," said Raggedy Ann. "And, you know, it is not how we look that is important. What really counts is to be as sunny as possible inside; then no one stops long to look at the outside."

41

"Yes, indeed, Raggedy Ann," agreed Raggedy Andy. "An old, unpolished violin may hold the sweetest music, and the loveliest of pearls may be found in the shell of the roughest oyster."

THE BROWNIE'S KISS

FLOWING LAZILY through the Happy Meadow was a small brook whose waters were so clear that Raggedy Ann and Raggedy Andy had named it the Looking-glass brook. Flowers grew on both sides of it, making a many-colored frame for the silvery brook, and at one place was a row of yellow-red lilies, usually called Tiger lilies, nodding in the sunshine.

Raggedy Ann and Raggedy Andy noticed the pretty lilies and stopped to watch them bowing to one another. The soft, gentle breeze blew on them and made their green dresses rustle like Grandmother's

old silken skirt. And the Raggedys could also hear
a sound as of Fairies whispering.

"How lovely the lilies are!" Raggedy Ann softly
said. "They seem to make you want to be ever so
quiet, as if you were trying to hear beautiful music
coming from far, far away."

"Indeed, the scent of the flowers is part of Nature's
beauty," a tiny voice said to the Raggedy dolls. "Just
as is the music of all the creatures."

Then the Raggedys saw a little creature spring
from the ground and sail up to the nodding lilies.
Each lily received a touch from the little creature,
and it seemed to the Raggedys as if each lily nodded
'thanks.

"Yes." The little creature laughed a bell-like

laugh. "Truly, their perfume is the message that the flowers send to tell us of Nature's great wonder and beauty. Think of the fragrance of the tiny little violet who spends his time hidden away down beneath the tall grass. The perfume the tiny violet sends out on the gentle breeze is the violet's message. And what wonders and loveliness it would tell of if folks could only understand."

"It makes my candy heart feel almost as if it would burst out of the stitches in my rag body," said Raggedy Ann. "Nature has such wonderful things to tell us in such beautiful ways, if we can only try to understand."

"But why did you spring up and touch each lily?" Raggedy Andy asked the little creature, for he was still thinking about that.

"Do you mean to say that you did not see what I did?" the little creature laughingly asked.

"We have only shoe-button eyes," Raggedy Andy answered. "And although we usually see very, very well with them, we couldn't see this time. Maybe you were too quick for our eyes."

"Now, watch again." The little creature laughed, sprang up and again touched each nodding lily.

"I see!" Raggedy Ann sang out as she clasped her rag hands together in amazement.

"So do I," Raggedy Andy chimed in. "There is a tiny brown spot on every lily just where you kissed it."

"Oh, now I know what you are!" Raggedy Ann laughed happily.

45

"What am I?" the little creature asked, his tiny eyes twinkling merrily.

"You are a Brownie, that's what!"

"Really?" Raggedy Andy could scarcely believe it. "We have always wanted to see a Brownie, haven't we, Raggedy Ann?"

"Yes, we have whispered about it many times at night," said Raggedy Ann.

"Well, I'm not much to see!" The little creature laughed. "I'm as brown as Jenny Wren, but I am much smaller than she is."

Raggedy Ann said, quite seriously, "Even though your coat is as brown as Jenny Wren's, I think that, inside of you, there must be a silvery star-twinkle. And I imagine you must understand the message of the flowers."

"Yes, I do understand it," the little Brownie replied. "But this is a message that each of us has to learn to understand for himself." And with this, he got ready to fly off once more.

Raggedy Andy, however, had one more question to ask him hurriedly: "Do you leave a brown spot wherever you touch anything?"

"Oh, no!" the little Brownie answered. "I leave a brown spot only when I kiss someone I like very much."

"How happy all the children will be to learn this!" exclaimed Raggedy Ann.

"But why?" Raggedy Andy asked, somewhat puzzled.

"Oh, Raggedy Andy, don't you see why they will

WORTH
GRUELLE

47

be glad to know? Just think of all the children who have freckles and are unhappy about them!"

"Oh, now I see!" Raggedy Andy cried as he stood on his rag hands and kicked his heels in the air. "Every little freckle is a sign that a Brownie has kissed a child he loves!"

Mister Skeeter Hawk

"LET'S PICK a bouquet of buttercups," Raggedy Ann said to Raggedy Andy as the two came to a spot beside the lazy Looking-glass brook where the yellow flowers grew in great patches.

"That will be nice," Raggedy Andy agreed. "Then I can make a crown of them for you, and you can pretend you are a Fairy Princess."

So, laughing and talking, the two rag dolls walked out among the pretty buttercups and began gathering a bouquet. Soon, hundreds of tiny mosquitoes flew up around their faces and hummed near their shoe-button eyes.

"You look as if you had a very dirty face, Raggedy Ann," said Raggedy Andy when he saw so many mosquitoes gathered on her face.

"So do you, Raggedy Andy," Raggedy Ann laughingly replied as she drew close to him, to watch the tiny insects better. "Look, they are standing on their heads!" She laughed as she watched the mosquitoes push their sharp-tipped noses through the soft material of which Raggedy Andy's face was made.

"And they all hold their back feet up in the air and wave them. Maybe that is their way of giving us kisses," Raggedy Andy said.

"No, I do not believe they are kissing us," Raggedy Ann said. "I have heard the folks talk of them many times when I have been taken along on a picnic. I know that whenever a mosquito did this same thing to any of the real-for-sure folks, it left a bump, and the folks smacked the mosquitoes with their hands. No, the folks did not like it at all!"

"Perhaps we had better smack them with our hands," Raggedy Andy suggested.

"Oh, no," Raggedy Ann hastened to say. "You see, they do not raise any bumps on us, for our bodies are made of cloth and stuffed with nice clean white cotton, and it doesn't hurt a bit."

"No, it doesn't hurt at all," Raggedy Andy agreed. "I can't even feel them."

But suddenly he did feel something strike gently at his back, and then he heard the whirring of wings. Looking around, he saw what looked like a toy airplane hovering in the air. As he called Raggedy Ann's attention to it, the toy airplane darted this way and that so quickly, the Raggedys could scarcely follow its movements.

"Aha! All of the mosquitoes have disappeared!" Raggedy Ann exclaimed as the toy airplane flew before him and seemed to hang in the air, its transpar-

ent wings fluttering so quick they looked still.

Raggedy Ann held up her hand and said to the insect, "Come and rest upon my hand."

"It may bite you," Raggedy Andy teased.

"No, I shan't bite you," the toy airplane said as it came to rest upon Raggedy Ann's soft white cotton hand. "I bite only mosquitoes."

"It wouldn't hurt even if you did bite me," Raggedy Ann told him. "Raggedy Andy was only fooling."

"Did you drive away all of the mosquitoes, Mister What-is-your-name?" Raggedy Andy asked.

"I'm a mosquito hawk," the creature replied. "Although some folks call me a dragonfly or a snake-feeder. But I do not feed snakes. I just eat all the mosquitoes I can find and—" the mosquito hawk laughed— "the more I can find, the more I can eat."

"Mosquitoes are a nuisance to real people," Raggedy Ann said. "I should think everyone would love you for getting rid of so many mosquitoes."

"Maybe folks do not love me because they do not

know how much good I do in getting rid of mosquitoes," the mosquito hawk said. "Anyway, many children try to hit me with sticks and things, and many
of my family have been hurt by small boys.

"Why, once I flew into a house when the screen
door was open, and the whole family chased me
around all day trying to hit me with fly-swatters and
folded newspapers, but I was too fast for them. And
that night I stayed in the house and caught about
thirty mosquitoes who were biting the folks. Once
during the night I heard the baby crying, and as I
flew above his crib I saw old Granpa Skeeter standing
on his head biting the baby's soft arm. So I just said,
'*GOBBLE*' and old Grandpa Skeeter will never bite
anyone again!"

"How grateful the folks must have been for what
you did!" said Raggedy Ann. "I should think people
would have a mosquito hawk in every house."

"Yes," the mosquito hawk agreed, "but, you see,
most people do not know how we help them. They
think because we scoot about over the waters and

over the marshes and boggy places that we feed snakes. And, of course, that is very silly."

With that, the mosquito hawk darted away, looking for more mosquitoes. And as Raggedy Ann watched him, she mused, "Hm, I guess most people do not know what a friend Mister Skeeter Hawk is, and how helpful he is to them."

Raggedy Andy suggested, "Very often we do not know how many creatures and even people do kind things for us in quiet ways."

And as Raggedy Ann started to pick more of the lovely, golden buttercups, she added, "But it is fun to make other people happy even if they do not know we are doing it!"

THE GRASSHOPPER FAMILY

RAGGEDY ANN and Raggedy Andy were sitting near the little home of Mr. and Mrs. Gregory Grasshopper, when the Grasshoppers came down the path pushing a tiny green-leaf baby carriage. Finding Raggedy Ann's apron right in their way, Mr. Grasshopper pushed and pushed until he had wheeled the carriage right up onto Raggedy Ann's lap!

"Here is the young Grasshopper family out for a walk." Raggedy Ann laughed as she smoothed her apron so that Baby Grasshopper would not tip out of the baby carriage.

"Why don't you let Baby Grasshopper get out of the baby buggy and play on Raggedy Ann's nice, clean, soft apron?" Raggedy Andy asked.

"That would be nice," Mrs. Gregory Grasshopper squeaked in her tiny grasshopper voice. With this, she lifted Baby Grasshopper out of the buggy and placed her on Raggedy Ann's apron.

"How old is she?" inquired Raggedy Ann.

"Just a week old yesterday," Mrs. Grasshopper proudly replied.

"She's very spry for her age." Raggedy Andy laughed as Baby Grasshopper kicked both hind feet and jumped as high as the top of Raggedy Andy's hat.

"We have to keep her tied in the baby buggy," Mrs. Grasshopper said as she hopped over to where Baby Grasshopper had fallen in the grass and was kicking her feet in the air.

"If we didn't tie her in," Mr. Grasshopper went on to explain, "she'd be hopping out all the time and we would spend most of the day hunting for her in the grass at the side of the road. You see," he added, "she doesn't know how to use her legs yet and she just jumps helter-skelter and bumps into everything that happens to be in the way. See?" He laughed as Baby Grasshopper kicked and hopped right off Mrs. Gregory Grasshopper's lap and jumped onto Raggedy Andy's shoe-button eye!

But Raggedy Andy caught Baby Grasshopper before she fell into the grass, and he held her on his soft white cloth hand.

"Dear me," Raggedy Andy exclaimed as he looked closely at Baby Grasshopper. "I do believe she is chewing tobacco!"

"My goodness, yes," Raggedy Ann agreed, leaning

56

closer to look. "She has a whole mouthful of to-bacco."

Mr. Gregory Grasshopper hopped up onto Andy's hand and held Baby Grasshopper, crying, "I will have to punish her for doing such a thing." And with that he raised his front leg to spank the Baby Grass-hopper.

"Wait a minute." Raggedy Andy laughed and took hold of Mr. Grasshopper with his other hand. "You seem to be chewing tobacco too."

"And so is Mrs. Grasshopper." Raggedy Ann laughed.

"Oh, no, we are not chewing tobacco," said Mr. Gregory Grasshopper. "So I don't know where Baby Grasshopper could have learned such a bad habit. If I spank her, she will remember never to do it again."

"But it looks as though you are chewing tobacco, Mr. Grasshopper. I do not think it would be right to spank her for doing the same things she copied from you," Raggedy Ann said quite seriously. "She

WORTH
GRUELLE

57

does not know it is wrong when she sees you doing a thing."

"My goodness!" Mr. Gregory Grasshopper laughed. "Now I understand what you mean. The food that we eat makes us look as if we were chewing tobacco, but really we are not. Let me make sure of what is in Baby Grasshopper's mouth."

When he looked, Mr. Grasshopper found that it was not tobacco at all, but the same plant that he and Mrs. Grasshopper were chewing. Then he laughed and said, "Gracious, we all have made a mistake. But I should have made sure of what was in her mouth before I got ready to spank the poor baby. I am very sorry, Baby Grasshopper." And with that he tickled the little one with his antenna.

Raggedy Ann smoothed her apron so that Mr. Grasshopper might step right off and put Baby Grasshopper into her baby buggy. When she was tied in tightly, Mr. and Mrs. Grasshopper said good-by to the Raggedys, walked down the path, and soon disappeared under the overhanging grass.

When the Grasshoppers were out of hearing, Raggedy Ann laughed and remarked, "We were all foolish for not making sure what was in the baby's mouth. But Mr. Grasshopper especially should not have been so quick to spank the baby before he was sure of what she had done."

And Raggedy Andy thoughtfully added, "Yes, it is very easy to find fault with others instead of finding out what the truth is about them."

HELEN HONEYBEE

"HELLO!" HELEN Honeybee sang as she flew onto a tall flower near Raggedy Ann and filled her little yellow basket with honey.

"Hello!" Raggedy Ann and Raggedy Andy smiled. "You are busy every minute of the time, aren't you, Helen Honeybee?"

"Almost all of the time," Helen Honeybee answered. Then as her little yellow basket was filled to the very top with honey and she could get no more into it, she hung it up on a petal of the flower and sat down facing the two Raggedys.

"A very funny thing happened the other day," she said while she wiped her hands clean before combing her hair. Then she continued: "You know, we honeybee ladies go from flower to flower gathering honey. And when we have our little yellow baskets filled we fly straight home and store the honey in cupboards so that we always have enough for the wintertime.

"Well, the other day, I was on my way home after I had filled my little basket. But I stopped on a blade of grass to rest when I reached the edge of the deep, deep woods. And, do you know, right below where I was sitting someone was crying ever so softly. 'Dear me,' I said to myself, 'Who can that be?' And I climbed down off the blade of grass and walked toward whoever was crying. But I could see no one, though the sound of the crying came from an acorn. Imagine that!

"I walked all around the acorn, but I could not see any door at all, or any way that a creature might have got inside. Finally, I saw a tiny little round window up at the top of the acorn, and this window was stuffed so tight with bits of wood that I could hardly pull them out. But at last I got them all out. When I peeped inside I almost bumped heads with the littlest, smallest, teeniest Elf you ever did see. Why, he wasn't over a half an inch high!"

"Oh, he must have been adorable!" cried Raggedy Ann.

"I wish you could have seen him," said Helen Honeybee. "He was so tiny. Well, I started pulling him through the little window and had almost got him out, when I heard someone softly tiptoe behind me. The next thing I knew, someone had pulled my dress so hard that my skirt was almost ripped off! 'Here, you stop that!' I said. But the someone pulled all the harder until my apron was torn off. Then I felt someone hit me very hard, and then whoever it was let out a great howl. Just as I got the teeny-weeny Elf out of the window I quickly turned around to see who was making all that noise."

"Who was it?" Raggedy Ann asked with much curiosity.

"Ha, it was Snoopy Doodjinipper, the Witch!" Helen Honeybee answered. "When she had hit me, you see, she stuck herself with the needle I carry in my sewing bag, and there she was, screaming while she hopped first on one foot and then on the other, and putting her finger in her mouth every other minute.

"But the little teeny Elf was the most frightened thing in the world. He threw his tiny arms around me and cried, 'Don't let her put me in the acorn again!' I said, 'Of course I won't,' and then I told Snoopy Doodjinipper to stop hopping about so, and I would make her finger better. But she was so angry, she wouldn't let me help her. Instead, she went hopping down through the grass as mad as she could be. That littlest, teeniest Elf told me that Snoopy Doodjinipper had shut him up in the acorn because he went swimming in her little pond, and that he had been in the acorn for almost a week!"

"Wasn't he very, very hungry and thirsty?" Raggedy Andy wished to know.

"Dear me, yes," Helen Honeybee replied. "But I gave him my whole basket of honey to eat and then he was all right.

"I felt very sorry for old Snoopy when I looked in my sewing bag, for I found that the needle was gone, and it must have stuck in her finger. But she would not let me help her."

Raggedy Ann said, "But it was very nice of you to give all your honey to the littlest Elf."

Helen Honeybee buzzed happily. "I was glad to do that. But the nicest part of the story is yet to come. You see, after I had given the teeny Elf my basket of honey, I had to go hunt for more, and it took me a long time. When I reached home at last, my sisters met me at the door and asked where I had been so long. When I told them what had happened, they showed me fifty little acorn buckets, all filled with honey. Then they told me that while I had been gone, fifty of the teeniest elves had come to the door with the buckets of honey, saying they were all for Helen Honeybee!"

"Wasn't that nice," Raggedy Andy exclaimed, smiling.

And Helen Honeybee spread her wings as she said, "You see, the little elves made my kindness grow and grow!"

Raggedy Ann added, "If we want others to be kind to us, first we must do kind things for them."

"Hmmm! Hmmm!" Helen Honeybee sang as she picked up her little yellow basket and sailed away across the meadow, leaving Raggedy Ann and Raggedy Andy sitting there smiling happily at each other.

MRS. SNOOPY

"LOOK AT THAT funny little woman," Raggedy Andy whispered to Raggedy Ann.

"I've been watching her come along the path," Raggedy Ann replied. "Something seems to be bothering her."

The queer little woman was only about an inch and a half tall and she came walking along in a jerky sort of way until she got to Raggedy Ann's foot. Then, looking up, she saw the two dolls smiling at her.

"Why are you laughing at me when my finger hurts so much?" the little woman asked.

"We can't help smiling," Raggedy Ann answered. "Our smiles are painted on, so they can't come off till the paint wears off."

"Well, my finger hurts very, very much, and it is nothing to smile about," the queer little woman declared.

"We are very, very sorry about your finger," Raggedy Ann said sympathetically. "How did you hurt it?"

66

WORTH
GRUELLE

67

And the queer little woman told the Raggedys: "I live over in the deep, deep woods that are filled with fairies and everything, and in back of my house I have a clamshell. Well, when it rains, the clamshell fills with water and that is my pond which I use for washing and everything. I have a sign there that says, 'No swimming here,' but the little elves from the happy meadow come there anyhow to swim in it when I am away from home. And it makes me very angry."

"Do the elves make the rain water muddy?" Raggedy Ann asked.

"Of course not," the queer little woman answered. "But it is my clamshell and I do not want any one else to use it!"

"Hmmm," Raggedy Ann mused. "Did you hurt your finger on the clamshell?"

"No, that wasn't it," replied the little old woman. "Last week I caught one of the Elfin boys as he was swimming in my pond, and to teach him and all his brothers a lesson, I shut him up in an acorn for a week. But Helen Honeybee found him and let him out, and I was so angry that I hit her. But when I hit her, the needle in her sewing basket stuck in my finger. It has been there ever since. That's what is hurting my finger."

"Ho, ho," Raggedy Andy pointed out. "Your finger has been hurting you for several days, but have you stopped to think how the little Elfin boy's tummy must have hurt him for a week? He could not eat or drink while he was shut up in the acorn."

"I never thought of that," said Snoopy Doodjinipper, for this was the queer little woman's name.

"Well, it is not too late to think about it even now." Raggedy Ann laughed softly. "While you think, take the bandage off your finger, Mrs. Snoopy, and maybe we can help you."

Snoopy Doodjinipper removed the bandage and climbed up on Raggedy Ann's apron so that the two rag dolls might see.

"Yes, the needle is still there," said Raggedy Ann. "But we cannot pull it out because we have no fingers on our hands."

"Oh dear, what shall I do?" Snoopy wailed. "It feels as if it is going *'thump, thump, thump'* all the time."

"Just as the little Elf's tummy did when he was shut up in the acorn," Raggedy Andy thought to himself.

Just then Percy Pinchbug climbed on Raggedy Ann's apron and this gave the little rag doll an idea. Clapping her hands together, she called, "Here, Percy Pinchbug, will you please pull this needle from Snoopy's finger?"

Percy Pinchbug got out his pinchers and quickly pulled Helen Honeybee's needle from Snoopy's finger.

"Oh, now it doesn't hurt at all," said Snoopy Doodjinipper. "Thank you so much, Raggedy Ann and Percy Pinchbug."

"You are quite welcome," said Raggedy Ann.

"Very nice of you," said Percy Pinchbug. "But really you should thank Eddie Elf, for little teeny-weeny Eddie Elf sent me to pull it from your finger, Mrs. Snoopy."

"The teeny-weeny Elf that was shut up in the acorn?" asked Mrs. Snoopy, very much surprised.

"He is the one!" Percy Pinchbug replied.

"Dear me! I can hardly believe it," said Mrs. Snoopy. "I know how badly he must have felt in the acorn for a week, and here he has forgiven me for the way I mistreated him!"

"Eddie is a very nice little fellow," Percy Pinchbug said. "He and his little cousins help the little flowers with broken stems, and do kindly things for all the creatures living down beneath the grass. That is why the little elves are happy little fellows."

"Maybe that is why I am never happy." Mrs. Snoopy Doodjinipper wiped her tiny eyes with the corner of her apron. "Maybe if I would do kind things I would be happy too."

"Yes, indeed, you would!" Raggedy Andy laughed. "For every time you do something nice for someone, you feel a glow of sunshine inside you."

"Thank you, thank you," said Mrs. Snoopy Dood-jinipper. "I shall go right home and put a sign on the clamshell pond that reads, 'Everyone may bathe here'."

With this, she picked up her little skirts and went skipping down the little path. And Percy Pinchbug put his tiny pinchers back in his pocket and winked both eyes at the smiling faces of Raggedy Ann and Raggedy Andy.

The Magic Potion

"Rrrrr-rattle-de-dat!" Grampy Hoppytoad came up the litle path toward Raggedy Ann and Raggedy Andy, beating his little Hoppytoad drum.

"Here I am!" Grampy Hoppytoad said as he climbed up onto Raggedy Ann's apron and blinked his large eyes. "Open your mouths and shut your eyes and I'll give you something to make you wise." Grampy Hoppytoad laughed as he reached into his coattail pocket.

Both Raggedys laughed heartily from deep down in their cotton-stuffed throats. "We can't do that, Grampy," they said.

"Oh, that's so." Grampy Hoppytoad laughed.

"Your mouths are painted on and your shoe-button eyes can't close. I had forgotten. Well, well, now let's see what we can do. I have a magic potion for you, but you must take it like medicine."

"Maybe you can find a rip in our heads somewhere and push the magic potion inside," Raggedy Ann suggested. She and Raggedy Andy immediately lay flat so that Grampy Hoppytoad might search for a rip. But their heads were sewed up neatly and there was not a single rip anywhere.

"That's too bad," said Grampy Hoppytoad, "for with this magic potion you would be able to see all the fairies and elves and gnomes and everything."

"Oh, dear!" the rag dolls both said sadly. "We would like to see the fairies and elves and gnomes ever so much. Let's try to think of something."

"Whatever are you trying to do?" Grampa Hoppergrass asked as he came up the path on his way to the movies with Gramma Hoppergrass.

Grampy Hoppytoad told his friends that he wanted to give a magic potion to the Raggedys, so they might

73

see the fairies and elves and gnomes and everything, but he had not been able to think of a way to get the potion into the rag dolls.

"Oh, that is easy to fix!" Grampa Hoppergrass said. Then he told the Raggedys to lie down and stay still a moment. With his hind leg Grampa Hoppergrass sawed a wee hole in Raggedy Ann's and Raggedy Andy's heads, back up in under their yarn hair where it would not show. And, of course, since their heads were made of cloth and stuffed with soft white cotton, it did not hurt at all.

Grampa Hoppergrass' leg was just like a tiny saw, but neither of the two rag dolls had known this before. It took only a moment for Grampy Hoppytoad to push the magic potion into Raggedy Ann's and Raggedy Andy's soft cotton-stuffed heads. Then Aunt Sophia Spider, who lived close by, was called to sew up the holes.

When Raggedy Ann sat up, she gazed about her everywhere and breathed a long "Ohhh" of delight. The flowers looked more colorful than they had ever looked before. Even the grass was such a bright green that it made her shoe-button eyes want to blink. And the sunbeams falling everywhere over the meadow shone like beams of gold. But best of all were the lovely, dainty fairyland creatures playing about in the meadow.

"Isn't it beautiful, Raggedy Andy?" Raggedy Ann whispered.

"Indeed it is," Raggedy Andy quietly answered. "There are fairies everywhere, swinging on the blades of grass and flying around the flowers. Oh, thank you, thank you very much, Grampy Hoppy-toad and Grampa Hoppergrass and Aunt Sophia Spider!"

"You are welcome," the little creatures replied happily.

Raggedy Ann and Raggedy Andy could now see all the little fairies and little elves and gnomes, just as all the meadow creatures could see them. And for the first time the Raggedys were able to play games with all the fairyland creatures. When a swarm of tiny fairies swooped over the top of the grass and playfully grabbed Raggedy Andy's little blue cap, the two rag dolls laughed and shouted. They ran after the fairies as fast as their rag legs would carry them, but of course they could not run so quickly as the fairies could fly.

My, what great fun they all had. Sometimes the little fairies would let the dolls get so close, the Rag-gedys could almost reach Raggedy Andy's hat. Then with a merry shout the little fairies would whisk the cap high up in the air.

WORTH GRUELLE

75

When the little fairies had tired of playing with the cap, they brought it and placed it on Raggedy Andy's head.

"That was so much fun!" Raggedy Andy shouted. "When we have rested awhile, let's play it again."

"While you're resting, we'll show you a fine game," one of the tiny fairies cried, and with this, Raggedy Ann and Raggedy Andy were whisked higher into the air than Andy's cap had gone before. Then when they were 'way, 'way up above the great meadow and could see for miles and miles, the little fairies let go of the two rag dolls, who tumbled head-over-heels, faster and faster, until they almost touched the top of the grass!

Then the tiny fairies whisked them high in the air and did it all over again. Raggedy Ann and Raggedy Andy laughed loud with the fun and excitement, and the meadow echoed with the happy shouts of all the fairyland creatures and the two Raggedys. Truly, it was a happy meadow!

"It was just like going down fast in an elevator,"

Raggedy Andy said when the fairies had let the two dolls down again into the soft green grass.

"Or as if you were swinging very, very high in a swing—except it was much more fun," said Raggedy Ann.

"We'll show you plenty of fun the next time you visit us," the little fairies said, "but now we have to go to our work."

"My goodness!" Raggedy Andy exclaimed. "I didn't know that fairies ever had to work."

"We do not *have* to work," one little fairy said. "We love to work. And, you know, when one loves to work, then that means it is fun too."

"Yes, that is true," Raggedy Ann said to Raggedy Andy as the little fairies flew away. "When we do

things with happy hearts, it makes the hardest tasks seem play. But when we have chores to do and we sit and look at them, and put them off and grumble about them, then the tasks seem ever so much more unpleasant and they are ever so much harder to do."

HINKIE-DINKIE, THE MAGICIAN

"WHERE DO ALL the little meadow fairies and elves live in the wintertime when the meadow is covered with deep snow?" Raggedy Andy asked Grampy Hoppytoad.

Raggedy Ann, looking all round her at the happy meadow, could see the grass becoming brown already, and she could tell that the air had a chill nip in it. She and Raggedy Andy knew that winter would soon sweep in with cold winds and great drifts of snow. And although the snow was so beautiful to look at, when it came, it might be hard for the little creatures to keep warm and to get food. So that was why Raggedy Andy was asking the wise Grampy Hoppytoad what their friends would do.

"Oh, if you could just look down beneath the snow when it lies deep on the meadow," Grampy Hoppytoad laughingly told them. "You would see what a lovely place it is to live in, even in the winter. When the snowflakes fly down from the sky, the blades of grass bend over with the weight of the fallen snow,

79

and they keep the tiny paths and roadways of the meadow creatures clear. The snow is like a blanket, too, because it keeps the sharp cold winds from sweeping up the tiny paths, so the paths are not too cold. Of course, some of the fairies fly away when the birds fly south in the fall, but most of the fairies stay here all winter. Some of the fairies have homes down in the ground, with little fireplaces to keep them quite warm. And when the tiny meadow creatures get cold, as they sometimes do when there is not a covering of snow to protect their paths, then the little fairies or sometimes the elves invite the little creatures in to live with them. And a little fairy or elfin house, with a cozy fire going and everyone sitting about sewing, or playing games, or singing, is a wonderful, full-of-fun place to be."

"How pretty it must be with the shining white snow all above the little houses and streets," said Raggedy Ann, her shoe-button eyes dancing at the thought.

"Indeed, it is lovely," Grampy Hoppytoad replied.

"When the sun shines on the top of the snow, the little houses and streets look as if they had been painted with gold. But would you like to hear the story of what happened to me last winter?" he asked as he got out his pipe.

Both Raggedys said eagerly, "Oh, do tell us the story, Grampy Hoppytoad. We would love to hear one of your adventures."

And they snuggled together while Grampy filled his pipe, lighted it and took the first long puff on it. Then he began:

"I usually get pretty drowsy when it begins to grow cold. Sometimes I go to sleep right out on one of the paths. And that is what happened to me last winter.

81

WORTH
GRUELLE

82

I just fell asleep in the middle of a roadway. And when I awakened, for a while I did not know where I was. Everything was so strange to me, and I said to myself, 'Grampy Hoppytoad, you have never been here before.' And, sure enough, I never had been there before. I was right in front of a nice cozy fireplace and there beside me smoking his long-stemmed pipe was Hinkie-Dinkie who everyone says is a magician. I closed my eyes quickly and wondered how I would get out of his little house. You see, he lived down beneath the great tall rock in the center of the meadow, and no one I knew had ever been near his place, for some folks said he would change you into a different creature.

"Why—" Grampy Hoppytoad laughed— "some-

one told me once that he changed Charlie Caterpillar
into a butterfly. Of course that was nice for Charlie,
but we thought he might decide to change us into
things we would not like to be. So when I saw Hinkie-
Dinkie, my, I was shaking in my boots. I shut my
eyes tight and pretended to be snoring. And what
do you think?" Grampy Hoppytoad winked an eye
at Raggedy Andy.

"I guess he tried to change you into something but
couldn't," said Raggedy Andy.

"No, sir!" Grampy Hoppytoad declared. "When
I snored, Hinkie-Dinkie brought a nice soft blanket
and wrapped it around me, so that I felt warm and
comfy. 'There you are,' he said quietly. 'You will
soon get over that cold.' You see—" Grampy Hoppytoad chuckled— "Hinkie-Dinkie thought I had
a cold when I snored. So I opened both eyes and said
to him, 'What are you going to change me in to?' And
Hinkie-Dinkie said, in a surprised sort of way,
'Mercy me, Grampy Hoppytoad, Mother Nature
made you a Hoppytoad and that's what you will be

84

until your last day!' And he laughed so cheerily I knew he wasn't fooling me. Then he asked, 'Would you like a cup of honeydew tea?' So we had a cup of tea together while we smoked our pipes and laughed and talked.

"Then Hinkie-Dinkie told me that he had found me fast asleep on the cold path and had dragged me home, so that I would not freeze to death. And do you know, Hinkie-Dinkie had a whole houseful of poor little creatures. All winter long he took care of them until spring came and they were able to go out into the sunshine again.

"Well, when I told all the meadow creatures about Hinkie-Dinkie saving my life, no one dared to call him a magician, unless he meant something very nice by that name. For the little creatures and I found that he was always ready to help others just as he had helped me."

"Wasn't that a good story?" Raggedy Ann asked Raggedy Andy.

"Yes, indeed, I liked it very much," said Raggedy Andy as he stood and stretched.

Grampy Hoppytoad lighted his pipe again, for it had gone out while he was storytelling. Then, very thoughtfully he said, "It just goes to show that so many, many people, when we get to know them, are really kind and good. We should never speak ill of another person when we know what he is like only from the way he looks or from what others say of him."

Grampy Hoppytoad took a long pull on his pipe

as he said, "Hmm, many of the sweetest and most beautiful flowers grow from the ugliest little seeds, and we can never judge anyone until we know what is in his heart."

Sophia Spider's Spinning Wheel

"Oh dear, now just look at that, will you!" exclaimed Raggedy Andy as he twisted his rag head 'way around to look at the seat of his pretty blue trousers. "There's a great big hole where I tore my pants on that sharp stick."

"Oh my," Raggedy Ann sympathized as she bent to look at the hole. "It is quite a large one, and we have no needle or thread with which to mend it."

"Does it show very much, Raggedy Ann?" asked Raggedy Andy with concern.

"Well, quite a bit." Raggedy Ann laughed. "I can see your rag leg through the hole."

"I can feel the wind blowing through it, just as if

87

it were a little window." Raggedy Andy had to laugh. "Well, one thing is sure: it means good luck. For see, Raggedy Ann, the hole has the shape of a letter L."

"So it does," Raggedy Ann marveled. "It is an L and that stands for luck."

"Maybe we'll find a strange pocketbook filled with golden pennies that doesn't belong to anyone," Raggedy Andy suggested.

"Let's walk along slowly, and if we look very closely, maybe we shall find one," offered Raggedy Ann.

So, each with an arm about the other's shoulder, the two rag dolls walked through the happy meadow with their heads bent over and their shoe-button eyes looking closely at every inch of ground.

"Look out! Look out!" called a voice just ahead of them, which startled the two friends so, they almost fell over backward. There, a short distance ahead of them, was Sophia Spider, out on her front porch waving her little broom.

"I was afraid you might bump your heads into my house," she said.

"It wouldn't hurt us if we did," said Raggedy Andy, "for our heads are made of cloth and stuffed with nice white cotton."

"And our smiles are painted on," Raggedy Ann added.

"Well, well." Sophia Spider laughed, leaning on her little broom. "Maybe it wouldn't hurt your heads, but gracious, it would tear my house to pieces, that's sure!"

Aunt Sophia Spider's little house was built near the top of some ironweed. She told the two Raggedys, "It is very nice up here when the wind blows, for my little house sways gently back and forth and that puts me to sleep as soon as I get into my little bed."

"It must be very restful and pleasant," said Raggedy Ann.

"Oh yes, it is quite pleasant." Aunt Sophia Spider smiled. Thoughtfully she added, "If you were not

so large, I would ask you to come up and have a cup of tea with me."

"That is very kind of you, but I think we shall go on with our search for a pocketbook filled with golden pennies," said Raggedy Ann.

Aunt Sophia Spider picked up her head and asked, "Eh, what's that about a pocketbook filled with golden pennies?"

So Raggedy Andy explained about the tear in his pants that had the shape of a letter L which surely meant they would find something lucky.

Aunt Sophia Spider laughingly told them, "Maybe the L meant that you would be lucky enough to find someone who could sew your pants. Turn around, Raggedy Andy, and let me see that tear."

Aunt Sophia peered at Raggedy Andy when he turned, but she could not see the large tear. So she pulled a tiny silken cord and slid down in her spider elevator until she hung right next to the hole in Raggedy Andy's trousers.

Then she exclaimed, "Dear me, that is quite a tear!

You poor child, don't you have any mama to sew it up for you?"

The two Raggedys laughed at this and Andy said, "Neither of us has a mama unless you wish to call the lady who made us out of nice white cloth and cotton fifty years ago!"

"I guess I am Raggedy Andy's mother when we are at home." Raggedy Ann laughed. "And he is my daddy then too, for we often sew up the rips in each others arms and legs."

"Yes," Andy agreed. "Raggedy Ann sometimes has to sew on a leg because I tumble about so much that every once in a while I tear out all the stitches and a leg falls right off!"

"Doesn't it hurt at all?" Aunt Sophia Spider asked,

hardly daring to believe Raggedy Andy's story.

"Not one bit." Raggedy Andy laughed. "Nothing hurts us unless it is something we have done to hurt another person or creature."

"Oh, of course, that is different," Aunt Sophia Spider agreed. "When we do anything which makes someone else feel bad, that always hurts us inside."

"Raggedy Ann has a candy heart," said Raggedy Andy, wanting Aunt Sophia Spider to know how lovely Raggedy Ann really was.

"A candy heart. How unusual! But I can tell you are kindhearted too, Andy. And because I believe that you are a fine fellow, I am going to run up and get my spinning wheel. Then I shall spin a fine cloth right over the hole in your trousers."

It took Aunt Sophia Spider only a moment to run her little elevator up to her tiny house and come back down again with her spinning wheel. *"Whir! Whirrrrr! Whickity-whir!"* went the wheel, and soon Raggedy Andy's trousers looked as good as new.

"Thank you very, very much," Raggedy Andy said. "Maybe sometime I can help you in some way."

"Just do something kind for someone else." Aunt Sophia Spider laughed as she told them good-by. "Then I shall have the pleasure of knowing that, if I have made you happy, you can make someone else happy by doing something for them."

Raggedy Andy put his arm around Raggedy Ann as they walked along the path which led past the play house in the garden back of Marcella's house.

Raggedy Andy had just dropped to the floor to help Raggedy Ann down from the sill when they heard Marcella and Mommy come home from shopping.

Raggedy Ann said, "We are just back in time," as she and Raggedy Andy dropped in their little chairs as Marcella had left them. Their eyes twinkled as they thought of the adventures they had just shared.

THE

GRUELLE IDEAL

It is the Gruelle ideal
that books for children
should contain nothing to
cause fright, suggest fear, glo-
rify mischief, excuse malice
or condone cruelty. That
is why they are called
"BOOKS GOOD FOR
CHILDREN."